MR. CLEVER

by Roger Hargreaves

PSS!
PRICE STERN SLOAN
An Imprint of Penguin Group (USA) Inc.

Mr. Clever was quite the cleverest person ever.

The Cleverest Person in the World!

And, he knew it!

"Oh, I am so very, very CLEVER," he used to say.

To himself more often than not.

He lived in Cleverland, where, as you may know, everybody and everything is as clever as can be.

In Cleverland clever trees manage to grow apples and oranges at the same time!

In Cleveland clever flowers get up and go for a walk!

Oh yes, Cleverland is quite the most clever place.

Would you like to live there?

Mr. Clever does.

"Oh, I am so very, very CLEVER to build such a clever house," he used to go around telling everybody.

One morning, Mr. Clever was awakened by his special Mr. Clever alarm clock.

Not only did it wake you up by ringing a bell: it also switched on a light and said "Good morning" and made a cup of tea and showed what the weather was going to be and told you the time and showed you the date. It also whistled cheerfully while it was doing all that!

Mr. Clever yawned, got up, washed, cleaned his teeth (with his special Mr. Clever toothbrush, which squeezed toothpaste on to the brush out of the handle), and went downstairs for breakfast.

He popped a slice of bread into his special Mr. Clever electric toaster.

Which not only toasted the bread, but also spread it with butter and marmalade, AND cut off the crusts!

After breakfast he went for a long walk.

An extremely long walk.

In fact, such a long walk that he walked all the way out of Cleverland, although he didn't know it.

He met somebody who was also out for a walk.

Do you know who it was?

That's right.

Mr. Happy!

"Hello," cried Mr. Clever. "I'm the Cleverest Person in the World!"

"Oh good," said Mr. Happy. "Then you must be clever enough to make up a really good joke to tell me."

He laughed.

"Jokes make me happy," he explained.

Mr. Clever's face fell.

"I don't know any jokes," he admitted.

"Well, that's not very clever of you, is it?" said Mr. Happy, and went off.

Mr. Clever went on.

And do you know who he met next?

That's right.

Mr. Greedy!

"Hello," cried Mr. Clever. "I'm the Cleverest Person in the World!"

"Oh good," said Mr. Greedy. "Then you can tell me the recipe of the world's most delicious dish."

He licked his lips.

"I like food," he explained.

Mr. Clever's face fell.

"I can't cook," he admitted. "And I don't know any recipes!"

"Well, that's not very clever of you, is it?" said Mr. Greedy, and he went off.

In search of food.

Mr. Clever went on.

And who do you think he met next?

Yes.

Mr. Forgetful!

"Hello," cried Mr. Clever. "I'm the Cleverest Person in the World!"

"Oh good," said Mr. Forgetful. "Then you can tell me what my name is."

He smiled apologetically.

"I've forgotten," he explained.

Mr. Clever's face fell for the third time that morning.

"But I don't know your name," he admitted. "We've only just met!"

"Well, that's not very clever of you, is it?" said Mr. Forgetful, and he too went off.

Forgetting to say goodbye!

And so it went on. All day.

Mr. Clever couldn't tell Mr. Sneeze the cure for a cold.

And he couldn't tell Mr. Small how he could grow bigger.

And he couldn't tell Mr. Nervous what the secret of being brave was.

And he couldn't tell Mr. Topsy-Turvy how to talk the round way right.

I mean the right way round.

A not very clever day!

Not at all.

Not a bit.

As by now he wasn't feeling anything like The Cleverest Person in the World, Mr. Clever decided he'd better go home.

He passed a pair of worms who were having a chat.

"Who's that?" asked one worm.

"That," replied the other worm, "is Mr. Clever, The Cleverest Person in the World, on his way home to Cleverland!"

The first worm thought.

"He can't be that clever," he replied . . .

". . . he's going the wrong way!"